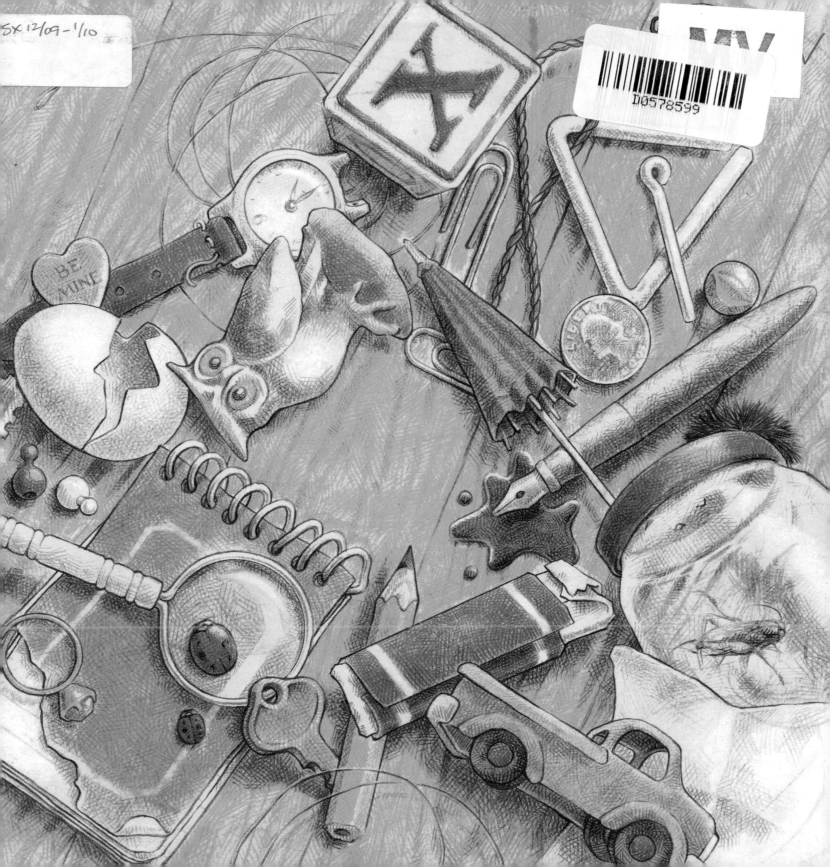

TREASURES
of the HEART

Written by Alice Ann Miller

Illustrated by K.L. Darnell

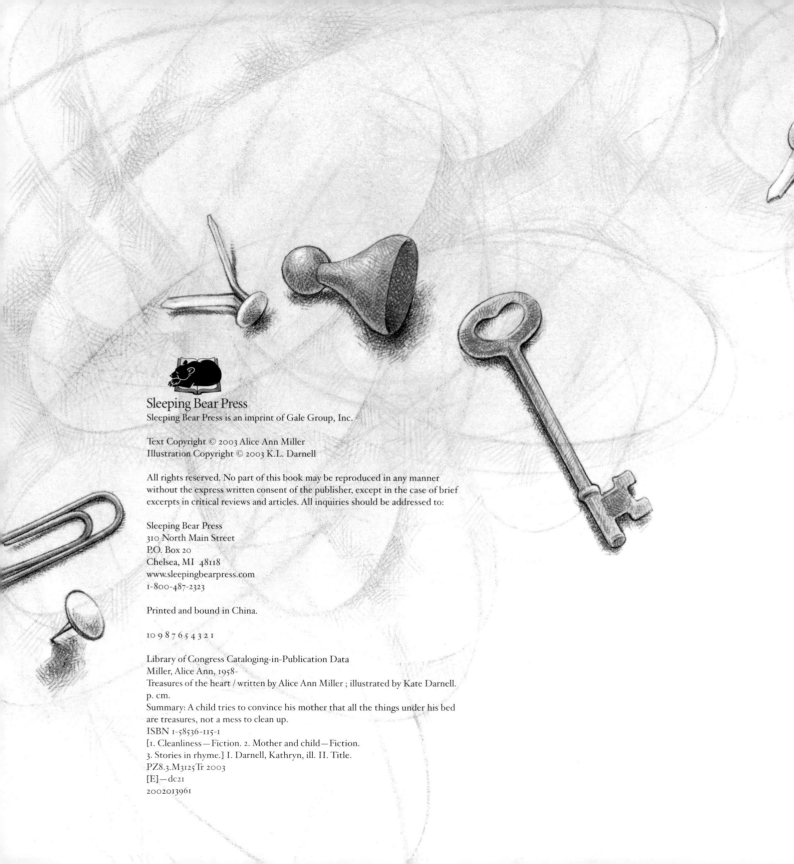

Sleeping Bear Press

Sleeping Bear Press is an imprint of Gale Group, Inc.

Sleeping Bear Press
310 North Main Street
P.O. Box 20
Chelsea, MI 48118
www.sleepingbearpress.com
1-800-487-2323

Printed and bound in China.

10 9 8 7 6 5 4 3 2 1

Library of Congress Cataloging-in-Publication Data
Miller, Alice Ann, 1958-
Treasures of the heart / written by Alice Ann Miller ; illustrated by Kate Darnell.
p. cm.
Summary: A child tries to convince his mother that all the things under his bed are treasures, not a mess to clean up.
ISBN 1-58536-115-1
[1. Cleanliness—Fiction. 2. Mother and child—Fiction.
3. Stories in rhyme.] I. Darnell, Kathryn, ill. II. Title.
PZ8.3.M3125 Tr 2003
[E]—dc21
2002013961

Tredsure ♡ xxx ooo

To my husband Charlie and our children, Adam, Drew,
Dustin, and Hannah, for their love, support, and faith in me.
To my mom for leaving me a legacy of dreams, and to Rita,
for helping me believe that I could make them come true.

They are truly the most cherished treasures of my heart.

—Alice Ann Miller

To Diana, treasured friend.

—K.L. Darnell

Come along with me to see,
the greatest treasure that will ever be.
It's not in chests on pirate ships
or in your favorite birthday wish.

It's buried deep and very safe.
I have it in my special place.
Come along, it's through this door.

Crawl with me along the floor.

We're getting closer. Watch your head.
Yes! Here it is, beneath my bed.

A paper clip,
    a potato chip,
        a broken pen,
            and three toy men.

Don't move that fuzz!
It's there because
it helps me hide the loot!

Let's see...

A coffee can
a rubber band
and...

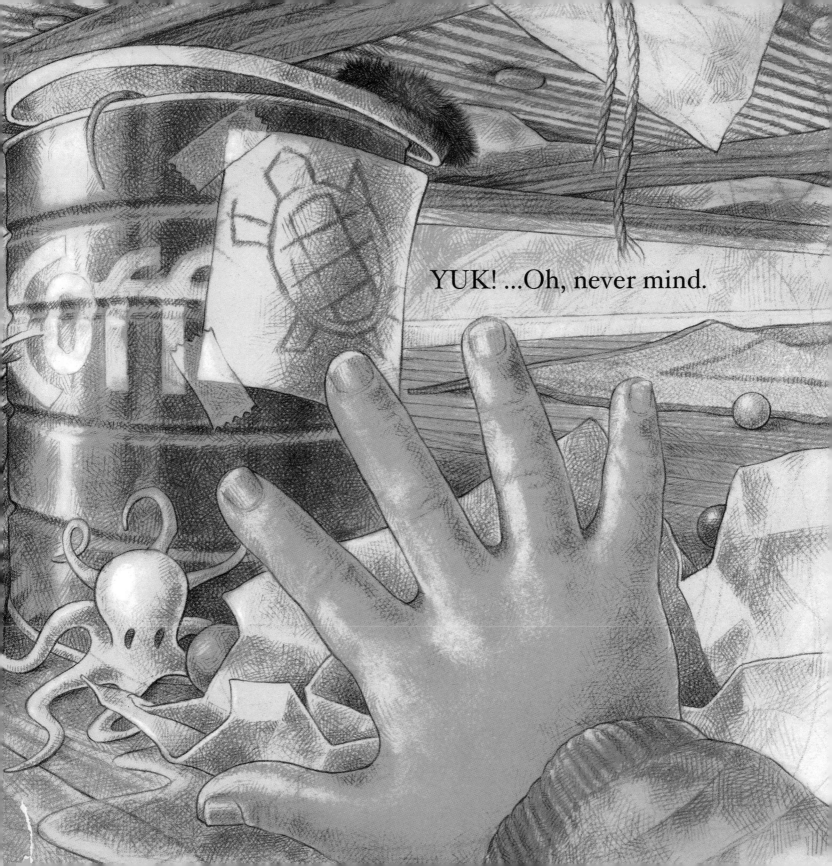

A yellow sock
my lucky rock

let's see what YOU can find.

My favorite car,
my cricket jar,
a two-year-old bird's nest.

A peach pit,
one pointed stick.

What do you mean?
"This is a mess!"

For everything that's under here,
There's a story I could tell.
I've collected all these treasures
and I've kept them very well.

When I couldn't save the whole,
I stored away a part.
Everything you see here
is a treasure of my heart.

No one but you has ever seen
the wonders I've just shared.

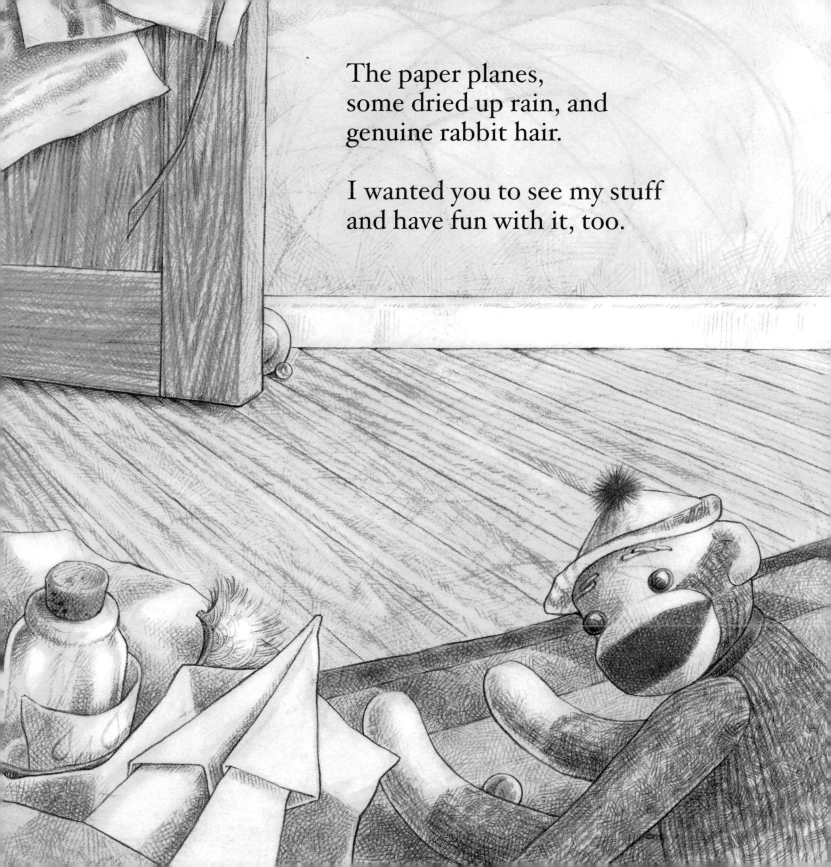

The paper planes,
some dried up rain, and
genuine rabbit hair.

I wanted you to see my stuff
and have fun with it, too.

You wouldn't want to break my heart
and throw it out...

Mom? Would you?

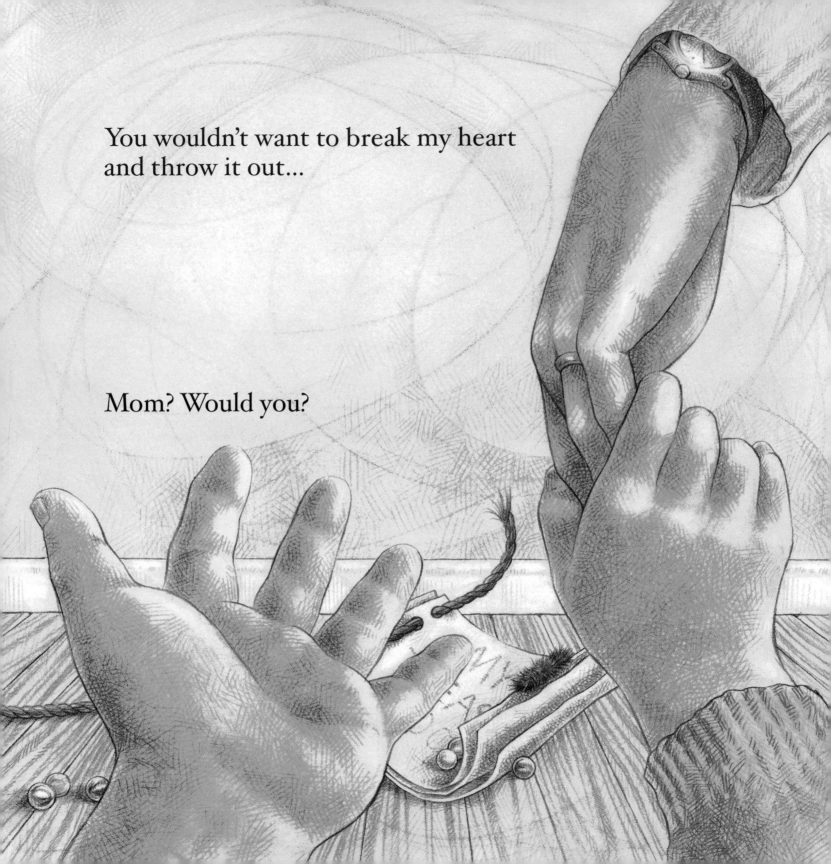